OUT OF THE TUNNEL

THE **RED** ZONE

OUT OF THE TUNNEL

PATRICK JONES

MINNEAPOLIS

Darby Creek
A division of Lerner Publishing Group, Inc.
241 First Avenue North
Minneapolis, MN 55401 USA

For reading levels and more information, look up this title
at www.lernerbooks.com.

The images in this book are used with the permission of: © Mike Powell/
CORBIS, (football player); © iStockphoto.com/mack2happy (grass).

Main body text set in Janson Text LT Std 12/17.
Typeface provided by Linotype AG.

Library of Congress Cataloging-in-Publication Data

Jones, Patrick.
        Out of the tunnel / by Patrick Jones.
            pages   cm. — (The red zone, #1)
        Summary: When Brian attains his goal of being a starter on the Troy,
    Ohio, Central High Trojan football team, as was his father, he enjoys new
    privileges but is exposed to terrible behavior that adults tolerate because
    "boys will be boys."
        ISBN 978-1-4677-2126-4 (lib. bdg. : alk. paper)
        ISBN 978-1-4677-4649-6 (eBook)
        [1. Football—Fiction. 2. Conduct of life—Fiction. 3. Fathers and
    sons—Fiction. 4. High schools—Fiction. 5. Schools—Fiction. 6. Family
    life—Ohio—Fiction. 7. Ohio—Fiction.] I. Title.
    PZ7.J7242Out 2014
    [Fic]—dc23   2013034230

Manufactured in the United States of America
1 – SB – 7/15/14

1 / THURSDAY, JUNE 7—
LAST DAY OF SCHOOL

"You got it?" Dad asked like a kid on Christmas morning. *It*, of course, was the football handbook for the upcoming season. No matter that today was June 7, the last day of school. Dad's mind was on Troy High football. Check that, he was always thinking about football. So was I.

"Most of it." I gave him the *Troy Central High School Trojan Football Player and Parent Handbook.*

"Most?" His smile vanished. *Most, some,* and

maybe were not words in Big Bill Norwood's vocabulary. Dad's a seal-the-deal, all-or-nothing kind of guy.

"There's just a few details to work out about the preseason games, I guess."

"Well, Bill—I mean Coach Zachary—will take care of that, I'm sure," Dad said. My dad and Coach Zachary played football together at Troy High on the team. Not a team, but *THE* team.

Dad reviewed the schedule. Practice began in ten days: conditioning, then skill camp, and then weights. It was T-shirt weather outside, but Dad and I both yearned for helmets, pads, and cleats.

"So there's a fee for conditioning now?" he said.

I shrugged. A fee didn't matter. With football, money was no object. It had been that way since fourth grade and Half Backs, Coach Zachary's youth football camp. Dad, along with other members of *THE* team, had served as coaches.

"Now, Brian, about skills camp."

"What about it?" I asked. And waited for an answer. Dad was in sales, so a quick answer was his stock-in-trade, but there was just silence. We sat on the big porch in the backyard. He drank coffee as always. Diet Dew was my stock-in-trade.

"Dad?" More silence. I checked my phone. I'd missed a call from Dylan Davis, my best friend and a fellow Trojan footballer. We'd both earned varsity letters as sophomore starters: Dylan at guard and backup fullback, me at linebacker. Best friends off the fields, we often banged helmets in practice.

"Brian, I couldn't be prouder of you starting last year, but for this season, I have an idea."

"Okay." I wasn't sure where this was going, but I knew where I was going: Ohio State, football scholarship, like Dad. Then, unlike Dad, the pros—hopefully, the Bengals. A true high school star, Dad had washed out at OSU, both on and off the field. So he pushed me hard on the gridiron, while Mom pressed me in the classroom. As a teacher, it came natural to her.

Dad set down his coffee and picked up an-always-at-the-ready football from the porch. He walked slowly into our big backyard, site of many a Norwood family football game. (Tackle, never touch.) I gulped the last drops of Diet Dew and followed him without a word.

"I'm not sure linebacker is the best showcase for you."

I wanted to argue: linebacker was *the* football position. It combined size, speed, and smarts. Hundreds of hits flashed through my mind— football at its purest.

Dad tossed the ball toward me, high. I snared it effortlessly.

"I see weakness in fullback."

I tossed the ball softly back. "Dylan's solid. He'll do fine." Dylan got minutes as a guard, but by end of the year, he was taking downs and gaining yards as full-back. With so many senior starters graduated and a weak group of juniors moving up, we knew we'd keep our starting spots.

"I agree. He's got potential." The ball came back to me, harder. "What about tight end?"

"What about it?" Tight end was now senior Mike Miller's spot. A good but not great player.

"Like linebacker or quarterback, tight end

requires the best athlete on the field," Dad said. When Dad played, Troy High was smaller. The best players had played on both offense and defense. His positions? Linebacker and quarterback. "And you're the best athlete on the team."

"Shane would disagree." Shane was quarterback and the best athlete. Just ask him.

I threw the ball back. Dad caught it with one hand. "At tight end, you can show your skills: running, receiving, and blocking. It's a good position for you. Better than linebacker. Safer too."

I'd played tight end in junior high but liked linebacker better. "Mike's pretty good."

The ball came back hard, right in the chest. I winced. "You're better than him, Brian."

I cradled the ball. For a second, I allowed myself to see it: catching the winning pass, the crowd yelling, cheerleaders leaping, and Dad beaming with pride. For my friends, I knew that's why they played: the chance at glory. For me, it wasn't about glory but the game itself.

"I'll talk to Coach Zachary. Coach Colby won't be happy losing you, but—"

"He's never happy," I interrupted.

Dad laughed. Colby was the defensive coach. A real hard case.

Dad motioned for me to throw him the ball, but I held onto it. "You're sure about this."

"Look, Brian, you've got to understand this is what's best for you. And the team."

I tossed the ball back. It fell short. Dad frowned at imperfection even in backyard catch.

"Being on offense *and* a receiver gets you in the center of the action, Brian."

And center of attention, I thought. *I'm not so sure about that. I don't mind being outside.*

"And unless things have changed since I played, there are other benefits." The ball came back to me in a perfect spiral that would make Shane green as grass. "You know what I mean."

I did, but I didn't say so. The Big Six. Everyone knew, but nobody said it out loud.

"So, we're agreed. You'll make the switch. Remember, it's for the good of the team," Dad said. "The Norwood family will always do what is best for Troy football and Trojan pride."

I smiled at Dad, but my mind traveled to the

scrapbooks that sat in his trophy case like holy books. The books contained every game program, every story clipped from the newspaper, and every flyer promoting the Friends of Troy Football Kickoff Carnival since grandpa Chuck played fifty years ago. My house acted as the Troy Central High Trojans football museum.

"Pass it!" he said.

I did as I was told, as always. Dad held the ball and my fate in his hand. I might change positions, but the bigger changes might be off the field. I wouldn't be an outside linebacker; instead, I'd be on the inside. Not just part of the offense but part of the Big Six.

2 / MONDAY, JUNE 18—
FIRST DAY OF CONDITIONING

"Is Devon here?" Mike asked. He stood with me, Terry, and Dylan outside the locked gates to Willard Auto Parts Field, formerly Trojan Field until Dad's boss bought naming rights.

"That would mean being on white people time," Terry joked. None of us laughed. I guessed Terry hadn't learned that unlike the people at his old school, the evil empire of Athens High, Coach Z didn't tolerate that kind of racist nonsense. The only color Coach Z wanted us to see was the brown of the football, the green of the turf, and the red numbers lighting up the scoreboard.

"If Orlando was here, he'd squeeze in." I pointed at the tiny space between the chain-locked gates. Wide receiver in fall, sprinter in spring, Orlando was rifle-thin and bullet-fast.

"Well, except his head," Terry said. We all laughed. We agreed on that. The only thing larger than Orlando's considerable talents was his colossal ego. Dylan joked that Coach Quinn bought a special oversized helmet for Orlando. "He'll be late too."

"Do you know who is running the first day?" I asked. Coach Colby and Coach Whitson took turns running conditioning camp, with Coach Z making an occasional appearance. Never knowing when Coach Z would drop in, kept all of us on our toes, including, I guess, the coaches.

"Witless Whitson," Mike said. Whitson made the call to replace Mike at halfback last year when Devon transferred before the season started. Even without taking part in the grueling football preseason program, Devon took Mike's job. Some guys, like Devon, just had *it*. I felt sorry for Mike, but then I was planning on taking his job this season, so not *that* sorry.

I wondered if Dad had already told Coach Z and Coach Whitson about his plan to switch me to tight end. With Dad being an officer in the Friends of Troy Football Board and an old friend of theirs, I knew they'd listen to him. I imagined the back-slapping-recall-the-good-times conversation. I avoided Mike's eyes, dreading the scene of him being told he wouldn't be starting at tight end.

"Real men would've climbed over!" Coach Whitson yelled from his SUV. He parked his Chevy Tahoe, honked his horn, and shouted, "Any of you ladies able to do some lifting?"

The four of us raced toward the parking lot. I beat Terry by one step, Dylan by two, and Mike by five. The tight end job was mine for the taking.

"Whatever you need," Dylan said.

"Lifting doesn't start until next week, but let's see if you ladies can handle some serious weight." Coach Whitson opened the doors to his

SUV. The seats were stacked high with boxes.

"What's this?" Dylan asked.

"While you were working on your tans and sipping Shirley Temples with your aunties, the coaching staff was hard at work." He lifted a box with ease. We all followed his lead. Mike tried to lift two but failed.

"Great hands, Miller!" Coach Whitson cracked.

Mike said nothing as he picked up the contents of the box: a thick notebook with a Trojan red and white cover. On the front it said, *Troy Trojans Conditioning Program—Hardened for Victory.*

"The coaching staff realized the reason you girls lost four games last year, including that fiasco to Athens, wasn't lack of talent but lack of conditioning. You were weak."

Dylan, Terry, and Mike muttered in agreement.

We weren't weak, I thought, *the other teams were better.*

"No excuses this year. We're going to work you like government mules."

More muttering from my friends, but I was distracted by my pain. The box in my hands felt light since other than a few of the linemen, I could move more metal than anyone, but my hands hurt. Maybe the others had been working on their tans like Coach said, but Dad had me working on calluses. He'd thrown—and I caught—more passes than a pretty girl heard in a year.

Coach put his box down, opened the gate, and led us onto the field. And as great as it was to walk onto the field, only one thing was better: coming out of the tunnel. When Mr. Willard bought the naming rights, he put in more seats, a better scoreboard, and a tunnel from under the stands onto the field like college and pro players had. When called, we'd burst out like cannonballs, running from the dressing room through the darkness of the tunnel then to the lit-up field under the crowd's roar.

I started back with Mike, Terry, and Dylan to get more boxes, but Coach Whitson called me aside. "Brian, Coach Z spoke with me. So, you want to try for tight end?" I nodded with vigor.

"Nothing gets handed to you. You'll need to work for it," Coach said, full throttle.

I rubbed the calluses on my fingertips.

"There are no favored nations in Trojan football, understand?"

Another nod, less vigor. We both knew that was a lie. There were three levels at Troy High: the Big Six, the rest of the team, and mere mortals who didn't play football.

We talked a little more, but pretty soon other players started to arrive. School had only been out a week, and yet here we all were. The goalposts were flames, and we were moths.

"BN, what's up?" Shane yelled from a distance. Devon and Orlando walked by his side.

Shane called everyone by their initials, except other members of the Big Six. He must have learned that from Coach Z, who called anyone who didn't start only by his jersey number.

I stumbled for an answer. Shane had it all: lettered in three sports, good grades, a hot car, and a hotter girlfriend. But like every hero, he had an Achilles' heel. He was the biggest jerk at Troy.

"It's hot out here. You look thirsty," Shane said as his pack closed in on me.

"I'm good." For some reason, this caused shivers of laughter among his group.

"Have some OJ." Shane handed me a big, clear bottle of orange juice. More laughter.

I gulped back the juice fast but spit it out even faster. "You got screwed!" Shane yelled.

Orange juice with vodka. A screwdriver. My cousin Stan loved them; I didn't.

"Word is you want on the right side of the field," Shane said. I nodded. "Keep your mouth shut, do as we say, and you got it made." Another nod, another gulp, another laugh.

3 / WEDNESDAY, JUNE 20—
FIRST DAY OF SKILLS CAMP

"Who wants it more?" Coach Z asked the huddled masses of players. Like conditioning last week and weight lifting next week, these "opportunities" were optional, except I'd never seen anyone but Devon and Terry make the team without suffering the summer away in agony.

"That's what it is about, kids." Coach Z paced back and forth—slowly, since he had little cartilage in either knee. Though it was a warm June day turning to night, he wore his blue and gold Trojan sweatshirt with Head Coach stitched on the sleeve. They'll bury him in that thing.

"We can improve your skills, build your conditioning, and help you add strength, but only you can bring out the best of yourselves." Coach Z's voice boomed over a sea of heavy breaths. The coach's welcome to us was a command to run the steps eleven times: nine for each regular season game and two for the playoffs. "We're in a competitive division, and in order for us to win, training and preparation are key."

This led to more nodding and muttering of agreement from fifty or so tired and scared faces, especially from the incoming ninth graders. Coach Z didn't break up skills camp or the first week of double practices in August into varsity and JV. He said it was to help the underclass build skills, but I guessed it was really a toughness test. Those of us, like Dylan and Mike, who played serious minutes as tenth graders, passed Coach Z's exam. As a PE teacher, like

Coach Colby, it was the only test Coach Z gave. Whitson taught business, a class all the football players took because it was an easy A. We all knew which teachers understood how the game was played.

Since Coach Z paced, he tended not to make eye contact. That was left to the other eight coaches. Mom liked to point out that Troy High had three times as many football coaches as school counselors and nine times as many as school librarians. As Coach Z continued to pace around, I thought I heard Shane, Devon, Orlando, and Terry whisper to each other.

When Shane laughed, Coach Z stopped talking. His angry glare only caused Shane to laugh a little louder. Like a chain reaction, other people started to laugh, including Mike who sat next to me. "Something funny, 54?" Coach Colby shouted. "Run off your giggles, now!"

And so it began.

———————————

Mike wiped the sweat from his brow to make room for more of it as he hit the steps.

"As the great Vince Lombardi said, 'Winning isn't everything, but striving to win is.' This has always been the heart and soul of Troy's proud football history." Coach Z was now in full-blown motivational halftime speech mode. "Football is a demanding sport of discipline and determination, requiring commitment and courage. It takes a dedicated athlete. Football is not for everyone, but playing football will give back to you far more than it will take from you."

As I watched Mike bravely battle exhaustion, I briefly questioned Coach Z's math.

"Football provides a sense of success and pride. It fosters self-assurance, bravery, and develops lifelong friendships. Being a football player is a state of mind and an honor that only a few share," Coach Z said and smiled. "Although winning is always the goal, remember what Vince Lombardi said, 'The harder you work, the harder it is to surrender.'"

Most players hung on to Coach Z's every word. Mom, who taught theater as well as language arts at Troy High, would joke—when Dad wasn't around, of course—that Coach Z would have made a great stage actor, but only if the play was nothing but monologues.

Coach Z stopped, pivoted, and faced the team front and center. We all looked to him for his wisdom and guidance. He was pompous but with purpose.

"Maximum effort, discipline, and sportsmanship matter most. They define success."

"And so does going undefeated and winning state," Dylan whispered for just me to hear.

"And getting lots of babes," Shane said loud enough for everyone to hear. Coach Z shot Shane another glare but didn't tell him to run steps. For all his high-minded speeches and Lombardi quotes, we knew Coach Z really believed winning was the only thing.

Coach Whitson gathered the backs and ends, while Coach Colby worked with the linebackers. Other coaches handled special teams, cornerbacks, and the linemen. Me being with Coach Whitson's group rather than Coach Colby's squad created more than a little buzz outside my circle. "So, let's see what you got. Groups of five on the field, now!"

I dashed onto the grass. Terry, Dylan, Mike, and two nobodies took positions. Coach Whitson hiked the ball to Shane, who dropped back to pass. Terry ran deep, while the rest of us sprinted ten yards, pivoted, and prepared to take the pass. Shane threw it to me, a perfect spiral.

"Good catch for a linebacker lady!" Coach Whitson said. "Let's do it again!"

Another lineup, hike, drop back, and toss. This time to Mike—well, Mike's feet.

"You got to catch those, 54!" Coach Whitson yelled. Shane shouted his agreement. As we concluded our final tosses, it became clear that Shane was making me and Terry look good, Mike look bad, and the other two kids look invisible. "Next group. Gary, you're in at QB."

"Thanks," I whispered to Shane as we walked toward the sideline.

"Nothing's free, BN." He wasn't even breathing heavy or sweating. "I gave you three perfect passes, now you got to give me and the rest of my crew something in return."

"What's that?" I whispered, dreading the request since I had so little to offer.

"Party this weekend before athletic code of conduct kicks in," Shane said and then motioned for Devon, Orlando, and Terry to join him. "I'll bring the girls; you bring the booze."

I had a hundred doubts but three questions. "Where? What time? How much?"

4 / FRIDAY, JUNE 22—
BEFORE THE FIRST BIG SIX PARTY

"Are you going to Shane's party?" I asked Dylan as we walked home on still aching legs from morning conditioning. The kind coaching staff let us take a Friday afternoon off, for now.

"I don't know, Brian," he answered. "What about you?"

On the field, Dylan was a leader, knocking down defensive players like a tank, throwing strong blocks so Devon could run free for serious yards. Off the field, he'd always looked to me.

"We've heard about these parties since seventh grade," I reminded Dylan. Troy was a small city, about twenty-five thousand people. It was hard to keep a secret. Yet these parties were like aliens: most everybody thought they existed, and some people even claimed to have seen one, but few actually had. At the big, adult-led bonfire parties Dylan and I went to last year, almost everybody on the football team attended except Shane, Orlando, Devon, Terry, and the senior starting fullback and tight end.

Dylan looked at the ground when we walked, not at me. "What if Coach Z found out?"

"He has to know," I said. Coach Z was such a control freak, it just made logical sense.

"Why do you think that?" Dylan asked.

"Coach Z was Big Six in his day."

Dylan laughed. "But what about the code of conduct?" To play sports, every student athlete signed a code of conduct. The code included provisions about sportsmanship, responsibility to teammates, and prohibited activities.

Partying was number one on a long list.

I kicked a small stone in front of me. "Technically, the season hasn't started, so . . ."

"So."

"So."

We walked in silence the rest of the way home.

―――――――――――

"What up, Little Bill?" Cousin Stan snapped. I'd shown up at his place unannounced.

"Nothing," I lied. He had to know I needed something, or I wouldn't be there. His father, Dad's brother Uncle Steve, was the family black sheep. Dad invited him to the reunions, but just for the joy of tackling him. Life had beat up on Steve enough; I don't know why Dad added to his pain.

"So how's football?" Stan opened the falling-off screen door to his trailer. Cars on nearby Interstate 75 buzzed past. Few slowed to give Troy a glance.

I gave Stan a quick rundown on the preseason so far, including my switch to tight end.

"That's a good move for you," Stan said as we sat in his small and crowded living room. On the wall were his varsity jacket, sans letter, and a replica of his Trojan jersey. Unlike his dad or mine, he had no trophies. Stan had been a second stringer, a human tackling dummy for starters. "You never looked like a killer out there at linebacker. You didn't take control of the game."

I agreed with him, which was another lie, but I needed his help more than my pride.

Stan rambled on about football, like everybody else in Troy. The town was too small for even a minor league or college team, so high school football was the only game in town. The game mattered so much to everyone, especially when we played Athens High. I asked Stan a few questions to help him recall his football glory days, or glory game, the ten seconds when he recovered a fumble on a punt return and ran it for a few yards. Once he was in a good mood, I was like a running back with the ball: I saw the opening and raced for daylight.

"Stan, I need a favor," I said. I never asked

anybody but Dylan for favors. I hated it.

"What can I do for you, Little Bill?"

For starters, I thought, *stop calling me Little Bill.*

I explained about the party. From the number of empty bottles and cans about, alcohol seemed dear to Stan's heart and home. "I was hoping since you're twenty-five, you could buy."

"A man could get in trouble. I'll need extra incentive." He rubbed his fingers together.

"That's the thing, I don't have any money." Football left no time for a part-time job.

"So, you want me to not only buy you beer, but pay for it myself."

"We need vodka too," I said. "For Shane."

Stan laughed. "Shane Hunter? The quarterback?" I nodded in agreement. "Little Bill, he'd better not hear you're dropping names like that. You'll never get in the Big Six."

The inner circle seemed to have its own code of conduct. I'd need to learn it, fast.

"If that's the case, I'll front the money, but you gotta pay me double after the Friend's Carnival. And that means you need to win the

Tunnel of Love bet." Like the Big Six, the Tunnel of Love bet was a Troy tradition I'd heard of, although Dad supplied few details when I asked.

"So, Stan, what was that like in your day?"

Stan breathed in deeply.

"All the Big Six guys put in twenty-five bucks, and it was winner take all," Stan said.

I paused, so he kept talking. "I didn't take part in the bet, of course, but like everybody on the team, I enjoyed the show." Stan laughed, rose from his chair, and walked through clutter to a desk. He opened the desk, moved around some papers, and then sat back next to me. In his hand was a brown envelope. He took out a piece of paper and held it up for us both to see. "You couldn't send photos by your phone in my day, so you had to print them out," he said.

The faded picture showed a girl with her face covered by her shirt. Next to her in the Tunnel of Love ride sat the guy who'd pulled up her shirt so she flashed the crowd. "You get in the Big Six, get your girlfriend to play along, win the bet, and you'll pay me back double. Deal?"

"Sure," I lied again. Even though I shook his

hand, I knew I'd never pay him back. I wasn't in the Big Six yet; I didn't have a girlfriend; and if I did, I wouldn't do that to her. What kind of person would do something like that? Oh, right. Troy football legend Big Bill Norwood.

5 / MONDAY, JUNE 25—
FIRST DAY OF WEIGHT LIFTING

"Are you happy with yourself, Norwood?" Coach Colby hissed like a broken hose. I lay on the bench under two hundred pounds of weight, so I couldn't escape. Nor could I ask him to get out of my sweaty face.

"Coach Zachary thought my move to tight end was best for the team," I answered.

"Blatnik has three left feet at linebacker," Coach Colby said. "He's got his two and one of mine kicking his behind." This caused lots of laughing, except from Joe Blatnik, who wasn't more than ten feet away. He shut his eyes tight and did his curls a little faster. Nobody worked harder in the weight room than Joe except Dylan and Mike, who were muscle-building machines.

"He'll get better," I said loud enough for Joe to hear. "And I'll excel at tight end."

"Just because your father is all buddy with Coach Z and on the Friends Board, don't—"

I pushed the weight up, hard and high. "That has nothing to do with my starting," I said.

Coach Colby snort-laughed. "Don't kid yourself, Norwood."

"You're wrong, and I'll prove it," I said, maybe telling a coach he was wrong for the first time ever. "I'll start because I'm the best. I'll help our team go undefeated and win state."

Another snort. "It's good to set high expectations. But don't kid yourself."

I started a second set of reps. The clanging weights drowned out Coach Colby. Unlike Coach Z, Coach Whitson, and my dad, Coach Colby didn't attend Troy High. He didn't get it.

"This is the best team we've had in years. If we beat Athens, then we'll beat everybody."

Coach Colby leaned over me, then put his hands on the weight. "That won't happen."

What is your problem? I thought but said, "We can't lose. Why do you think we will?"

He leaned closer. He'd had garlic at lunch. "If you go undefeated, don't you know what that does to all these people? If you win them all, then they lose it."

"Lose it? Lose what?"

"Then the team Coach Z, Whitson, and your dad played on isn't the only Troy team to go undefeated," Coach Colby said. He took his hands off the weight, which felt closer to my chest—or maybe it was just my heart beating so fast that it was about to leap out of my sweat-stained shirt.

"Looks like you'll start," Shane said after weights. To my surprise and delight, he'd invited me to join him, Terry, Orlando, and Devon in his hangout spot: the back of his Chevy pickup.

With a cooler full of fortified orange juice, Shane lounged in a lawn chair soaking up sun. "Miller's got nothing on you."

"Thanks." *For the compliment*, I thought, *and for making me look good*. I was doing better in skills than Mike, in part because I worked harder and was a better natural athlete. But I could tell, even if the coaches didn't seem to catch on, every pass Shane hurled toward Mike was just a little bit off.

"We're celebrating the fourth with a little Red, White, and Pabst Blue Ribbon," Terry said.

"Sounds like fun," I lied. My head still hurt every now and then from last Friday's party.

"You're not talking, are you, BN?" Devon asked. He'd been copying Shane's initials thing.

"Talking?"

"Off the field, what happens in Big Six, stays in Big Six," Devon said. "Got it?"

I nodded. I was in. We'd yet to play a down, but my head felt up in the clouds.

"So what about your friend, Dylan Davis?" Terry asked.

"That kid's gonna make it," Devon said.

"You see those blocks. He's concrete and—"

"You're a cement head, Devon. That's not what he means," Shane said before he sipped from his bottle of OJ. "What he means is, is DD going to be part of *our* team? What about it, Brian?"

6 / WEDNESDAY, JULY 4—
BIG SIX PARTY

"You're sure about this, Brian?" Dylan asked.

"Don't worry, it will be fine," I answered. We sat in his mom's Impala and waited for Stan to bring us the booze. This time, it was Dylan's turn to buy. He got some money from his dead-beat dad so he didn't need to make a deal like I had with Stan.

"I don't like it." Dylan tapped the steering wheel with his thumbs, including the right one that he broke in the last day of skills practice. He didn't tell anyone but me. What happens in huddle stays in the huddle. "I know the Big Six is tradition, but I don't want Coach Z to find—"

"I told you, Brian, he has to know," I whispered even though there wasn't a car in sight. "Coach Z was Big Six back in the day. Don't you see how he lets Shane get away with stuff?"

"What if we get kicked off the team?" Dylan asked. "I'm not like you guys. If I don't get a football scholarship, I won't go to college. I'll go into the army or end up working at Walmart."

"You won't get kicked off the team," I said very loudly as if to reassure myself. Football was a game of very clear rules with defined penalties: five yards for offside, ten for holding, and fifteen for a clip. But our Trojan team seemed to have two sets of rules: one for starting backs and ends, another set for everybody else. One group drew consequences; the Big Six did not.

"But I don't like to drink. It's all so stupid," Dylan rattled on. "I mean, that's time I could be studying the playbook or doing my homework once schools starts, and—"

"I bet once real practice starts, things will change," I said. "Now, it's just skills and drills, so I think Coach Z is just taking it easy before double sessions start in August. And then once school and the games start, I'm sure then he'll have a zero-tolerance policy like last year."

"But nobody who got kicked off the team last year was a back or an end," Dylan said.

"Well, I guess that was our good luck." We both laughed at other's mistakes. It was because Reggie and Titus got booted from the team for violating the code that Dylan and I got our minutes. I took Reggie's left linebacker slot, while Dylan spotted Titus at left guard.

"But what if that good luck runs out?" Dylan shouted over the rattle and hum of Stan's clunker Dodge pulling beside us. I stayed in the car, while Dylan finished the transaction.

I glanced at my phone. I'd missed calls from Dad, Mom, Mike, and Shane. By the time Dylan got back in the car, I was telling Shane we were on our way.

Unlike the last party at his uncle's house, when Shane, Terry, and Orlando brought girls, this was stag and out under the stars by Pillman Lake. Without the girls around, there was way more cursing, which seemed to make Dylan uneasy, but a little less drinking, which was fine by us. Shane played music out of his car speakers, which almost covered up how loudly everybody laughed at Shane's jokes or at the other guys as they made fun of our less talented teammates.

"Look, I'm Mr. Graceful, Joe Blatnik," Orlando said as he tripped over his own feet.

Terry added his Coach Z impersonation, complete with wobbly knees and worn-out clichés. "As the late, great Vince Lombardi said, 'I'm dead and I sure don't smell so good.'"

"Shane, toss me a beer," I yelled. Shane complied. I let the can smack me in the chest.

Around Devon, Terry, and Orlando lay six empty beer cans each. There were four between me and Dylan, only one his.

It must have been the laughter or the music

that covered up the sounds of the approaching feet. We didn't see our new visitors until Shane said politely, "Good evening, officers, wanna beer?"

7 / SATURDAY, JULY 14—
FIRST MEETING OF THE BOARD OF THE
FRIENDS OF TROY FOOTBALL

"Is that one of them?" Dylan pointed from my second-story bedroom window at the crowded back porch where members of the Friends of Troy Football Board gathered below.

"Sure looks like him." The person in question looked like most everybody else in Troy: very white, a little overweight, and standing quite proud of himself and his city.

"We got lucky," Dylan reminded me.

"You make your own luck," I said for the hundredth time.

"Now you sound like Coach Z."

The person Dylan and I had been staring at was Gary Sloan. Officer Gary Sloan. He and his partner, another former Troy Central High School football player, had let us off with a warning and a light punishment: they took the rest of our beer, although they left Shane's screwdriver gallon jug. Shane had been more than generous in sharing what was left over.

"Do you think we should be listening in like this?"

I shook my head no.

"But we're going to anyway, right?"

I nodded, and Dylan laughed.

"Hey, Brian, we gotta talk now while we got the chance," Dylan said. In two weeks, a lot of us from the team, including Shane and his crew, were going to a weeklong football camp at Ohio State. I'd gone every year since seventh grade, so I wasn't that excited about the training. I was interested, however, in the social opportunities that Columbus might bring a small-town boy like me. To hear Shane tell it, girls were like bees there and the football dorm was the hive. In the past, I'd sit up late into the night with my roomie—never Dylan, he'd never been able to afford it—playing video games and slurping down Dew like some dumb kid. No more.

I took Dylan up on the offer, and we swapped predictions for our coming season. Terry, who'd played at Athens in ninth and tenth grades, had given us some insight into their talents. As we talked, I wondered about telling Dylan what Coach Colby had said—that Coach Z didn't even *want* us to go undefeated—but I figured that was just bitter talk by someone outside the inner circle.

After plenty of laughs and more than a few drinks, the men—always men—of the Friends of Troy Football Board started their meeting. I'd never cared about the Friends before, but this year was different. The Friends looked after the starters, and I was a starter now.

The meeting started with a prayer, and then Mr. Willard spoke for a long, long time. You could tell that unlike my dad, he wasn't in sales, because he didn't know when to shut up. He droned on like some history teacher. I tried not to doze off until I heard the words "Tunnel of Love." No one mentioned the bet—would they speak of it out loud?—but they talked about the different rides in the carnival fund-raiser held the weekend before double sessions began. I listened a little more until they started talking about fund-raising.

"Let me know if anything interesting happens," I told Dylan, excusing myself and stepping outside of my room.

"Shane, it's BN," I said quickly into my phone. "No worries, it's happening again."

"Good. But the real question is are the two of you in or out?" Shane snapped.

"Um, we don't have that kind of money," I replied for both Dylan and myself.

"Ask your dad already." Shane sounded bored. "Figure it out."

I hedged, coughed, and made excuses. I'd told Dylan about the bet, and we decided there was a line and this was it. We'd party some, we'd joke along with Shane and the guys, but we were not doing *that*. I'd find some other way to repay Stan.

"What is your problem, Brian?"

"Look, I don't *have* a girlfriend, and—"

Shane cut me off. "You don't need one. We've got a new bet. Are you in or out?"

"What are you talking about?" Did he sense the panic in my voice?

"Just man up," Shane said.

"Look, Shane, I appreciate how you've helped me and Dylan, but—"

"It's not just me. Devon can try harder when Dylan blocks, so Dylan looks great. Or maybe Orlando and Terry don't get open, so I throw the ball to you more. Coach Z calls most plays, but I make it happen. Once practice starts in August, we can make you two look awesome."

"Like I said, thanks for—"

"Or we can make you look *bad*," Shane explained. "We're going to win with or without you, but with you, we might have a chance of going undefeated. I want that just to rub in Coach Z and Coach Whitson's faces."

"Okay, we're with you," I said, unsure of the words as they came out of my mouth. I wished that life had instant replay and I could change the decision I'd just made.

"Like I said, we do things a little different now, but your dad doesn't need to know that," Shane said, sounding more relaxed. "Besides, he was Big Six. He knows the rules of the game."

I started to respond when I saw Dylan's text: *Coach Z is talking & he's a little drunk, get back here ASAP*, Dylan wrote.

I told Shane, who seemed to get a kick out of button-down, always-in-control Coach Zachary slurring his words. "You need the money by the carnival. If not, you're out."

I agreed, hung up, and headed back toward my room. Down on the porch, these men who'd first met in high school ten, twenty, or even thirty years ago still remained friends. Troy football was the cement that bounded them then, now, and forever.

8 / SATURDAY, AUGUST 4—
FRIENDS OF TROY FOOTBALL CARNIVAL

"Dad, can I ask you something?" His early morning yawn transformed into a knowing smile.

"It's about the carnival and—"

Bigger smile, too big for his face. "And you're part of the six starting backs and ends."

"So, I need money for, you know." This was so odd. How could he approve of this?

Dad reached into his pocket and pulled out

his wallet. "What is it now, about twenty each?"

I stared at the floor. "Two hundred. A hundred for me and a hundred for Dylan."

"I didn't realize things had changed so much."

"Dad, it's something we need to do. You did it. Coach Z too. Now, it's our turn."

Dad's smile vanished, replaced by a lost-dog frown. My eyes darted back to the floor, in part to hide my knowing smirk. Mom was a language arts teacher and grammar queen, but I wondered if Dad noticed my pronouns: *we* and *our*. Whatever doubts I had about the Big Six, the bet, or any of it had washed away with the beer, the babes, and bonding that I did with Shane, Devon, Terry, and Orlando in Columbus. I was one of *them*.

"How will you win?" Dad finally spoke. "You don't even have a girlfriend . . ."

"It's different now." Just how different was something Shane had yet to explain.

"And more expensive!" Dad joked. "But you don't mess with tradition. You know I was the one who started that. It was our undefeated year when we won state, something no Troy—"

"I can't believe Mom let you do that to her," I said to stop hearing that story yet again.

"It wasn't your mother." His smile turned into a smirk. "It was Coach Zachary's sister."

———————

"We're in." I handed Shane the money. Dylan stood behind me, in but not in.

"Great," Orlando said to the crowd. He rarely spoke to me directly for some reason.

"But, Shane, won't Christina be angry—" I started.

Shane's laugher cut me off. "Like I told you at camp, that's not how we roll now."

"That's your old man's way of doing things," Devon said.

"We'll modernize the tradition for the twenty-first century," Shane said, although as he spoke, he seemed distracted by the Troy football fans flocking toward the carnival. The starting ends and backs sat in Shane's pickup, high above everyone. They all looked up to us: the Big Six.

"So, we'll break up into three squads of two people and look for girls," Shane explained.

"The younger the better," Terry said. "They're easy to convince."

"I'm not good at talking to girls," I said, "let along convincing them to flash people at—"

Everybody laughed but me and Dylan. "Brian, don't you get it. That's old school."

"Then what are we convincing them to do?" Dylan asked. I sensed fear in his voice.

"Brian, you, and me," Shane said.

"I'd go with Orlando," Devon said. "But two black guys together in Troy would scare these nice white country folks. DD, you're my blocker off the field too. Let's go meet some ladies."

"Let's meet back here at ten," Shane said. Lots of nods and grunts, just like a huddle. "Okay, let's go find some honeys for the pole of love."

"Pole?"

Once again, Shane replied to my question with a laugh, a grin, but no answer.

"Over there," Shane pointed at a girl siting alone. "Don't choke, Brian."

I nodded, ashamed. It had taken Shane all of ten minutes to snare the phone number of some incoming ninth grader. Despite being with Shane and wearing a Troy football T-shirt that showed off the muscles I'd been building all summer, I wasn't having any success. I liked girls just fine; I just couldn't talk to them, let alone get a phone number and invite them to a party.

"Look, Brian, maybe I was wrong about you . . ."

With a deep breath, I slowly walked over to a girl with dyed red hair. She sat alone just outside the midway games. She had one hand covering her face, the other clutching her stomach.

"Hey, you okay?" I asked from a respectful distance. She looked up at me.

"Brian?" she said softly. "It's Amber. Amber Murphy, from yearbook last year."

Shane had more or less said this was my last chance. Maybe I'd have better luck with someone I sort of knew. I took yearbook because it was also on the easy-A list, while people like Amber took it because they were into photography and journalism and stuff.

"What's wrong?"

"Nothing. Wait. I don't know, everything," she said through tears. "My boyfriend left, and he—"

Fortified with pickup lines from Shane, I pounced on her like she was a fumble. "I know this," I said softly as I sat next to her, hands in pockets to hide the shake. "If I was your boyfriend, you wouldn't be sitting alone and you wouldn't be crying. You're too pretty to cry."

The blush on her face matched the redness of her hair.

"You need to cheer up, Amber."

She wiped her nose with the sleeve of her white long-sleeve T. "How do I do that?"

"How do I do that, *Brian*?" My tone of voice was a balance of flirt and fear. She laughed. "There's a party tomorrow eve, you in?"

Amber smiled, nodded her head, just enough to say yes.

"Great. What's your number?"

9 / SUNDAY, AUGUST 5—
BIG SIX PRE-PRACTICE PARTY

"Any questions?" Shane asked me and Dylan. When neither of us responded, Shane walked back into the living room of his uncle's house. His uncle was out of town, and no one was likely to bother the twelve people in his house.

"I don't want to do this," Dylan said, but it was more like a whisper, given the background noise of music, laughter, and quarters bouncing into beer glasses.

"I know, Dylan, but we're here, so you have to pretend you tried. You don't need to win."

"I don't know how you can call any of this winning."

I said nothing as I reflected on the rules of the bet that Shane had explained to me and Dylan before the party started. What awaited Amber and five other girls wasn't a ride down the tunnel of love but a dance with a shiny metal pole.

"Man up, DD!" I said, which wasn't fair, since he'd been handling handoffs with a broken thumb. "We're not kids anymore."

"What are you talking about?" Dylan fired back. "That's all this is—kid stuff. It's not about football or anything important. Shane's a spoiled kid getting his way, and the rest of us are helping him. I'm done."

"Dylan, this is what we've talked about forever. You and me starting for Troy Central. And not just starting—playing positions where we can shine, on a team that might go undefeated. You're done with all that?"

Dylan grew quiet, especially given the contrast to the noise in the other room.

"Look, stay, play the game—you don't need to win," I said.

His lip curled in disgust. "Brian, trust me. Nobody wins on this. Nobody," he said as he walked not toward the back door but back into the living room, where games, girls, and opportunities awaited. Dylan was normally right about lots of things, but he was wrong. Somebody would win. Me.

10 / WEDNESDAY, AUGUST 8— FIRST DAY OF DOUBLE SESSION PRACTICES

"Gentleman, if you don't believe in heaven, you will after these next two weeks, because you're about to spend your time in hell," Coach Z announced to the fifty-plus hopefuls.

For the first time since fourth grade, I listened to a football coach's opening practice speech without Dylan by my side. He'd stayed at the party but left after I'd won the bet and maintained the Troy

Central High football tradition. I'd texted him many times since, but he hadn't replied.

"I recognize almost all of you," Coach Z bellowed. "That's good. It means you followed the coaching staff's instructions to attend conditioning, lifting, and skill drills."

"But if you thought that was hard, you ain't seen nothing yet," Coach Colby added.

"I've spoken with the office, and it seems a few of you can't follow instructions," Coach Z said. I tried to guess who he was looking at, but he'd yet to hit anyone with his death glare. "Before you can practice, you needed to turn in paperwork documenting you'd had a physical; the health questionnaire; the parental consent form; the signed code of conduct; and most importantly, a check for three hundred dollars made out to the school athletic department."

There was a small murmur, mainly from the kids without jerseys. Those of us from the team last year brought ours from home, sparkling clean. Not because we hadn't worn them all summer but because we knew Coach Z liked it that way. What he liked, we liked.

"We need that money to maintain the program," Coach Z said. "I know that is a lot for some of you, but it must be paid. Heck, I bet some of you can pay it out of pocket right now."

I was halfway into another seven a.m. yawn when I sensed something was wrong. I opened my eyes and Coach Z stood directly in front of me and repeated, "Pay it out of pocket."

Was the sun in his eyes, or did he just wink at me? Behind me, I heard Shane and our crew laugh.

"There's nothing funny about double sessions, ladies," Coach Whitson snapped.

"For you newbies, here's how we run things," Coach Z said as he walked away from me, allowing the sun to hit my face again. Did he know I won the bet?

"Double sessions are mandatory practices. In the morning, we start with conditioning, drills, and then we scrimmage, starting day one. You get better at playing football by playing football. But also by talking football, so we'll meet as a team, and then coaches will break you up and meet with you in smaller groups. There, you'll listen with your ears, not your mouth."

Each of the eight coaches stood behind Coach Z, posed like clones: arms crossed, lips pursed, and chins held high. They wore silver whistles around their necks, blue and gold Trojan football T-shirts, and steely glares of determination that would scare any child.

"Practice starts at seven, and we go until noon," Coach Z explained—spelling it out for those unable to read the handbook, I suppose. "We're back at five and go until eight. If you miss a practice, you'd better have a dead relative going in the ground or a broken bone sticking out of your skin."

A couple of people laughed, but I didn't. I thought about Dylan's broken thumb and our busted friendship. One would heal with time. What would it take to mend the other?

"Football is a sport of mental and physical preparation, so double sessions are key to preparing for the season," Coach Z continued. "You'll get a playbook at noon today. Between sessions, I'd better see your eyes focused on that playbook and not on your phones."

Terry jabbed me in the ribs with his elbow. "He wouldn't say that if he knew."

As Coach Z rambled on about teamwork, fellowship, and sportsmanship, my mind wasn't on him or even football. It centered on the photo on my phone, on the phones of each member of the Big Six. In that photo from the party, Amber clutched onto the silver pole with both hands. She wore a drunken stare on her face and nothing else.

11 / THURSDAY, AUGUST 16—
END OF LAST DAY OF DOUBLE SESSIONS

"Congratulations, Dylan!" I shouted as Dylan walked from our final practice. He walked with his head held high, having played the most minutes at fullback. Lots of Troy ninth graders walked head down, ashamed at not making varsity.

"I said congratulations, Dylan!" I ran to catch up with him. The equipment over my shoulder didn't slow me down. I'd grown stronger and faster this practice season, not just from hard work but also from getting my minutes. And the better I played, the more I played, thanks to the Big Six.

"What do you want, 75?" Dylan snapped when I caught up with him.

"What's with the attitude?" I asked. "I'm a number to you now?"

"It's a good number." Dylan smiled, in spite of himself, I think. Coach Quinn, who handled uniforms, had told me since I was playing tight end, I needed a new number. I chose 75 because of the interstate that ran through Troy. It was a prized pick for a junior like me.

I tried to smile back at Dylan. All I needed was for him to ask a question, and everything would be back to normal. He must have sensed it. "Are you guys all mad at me?"

I paused, but Dylan waited me out. He fiddled with tape around his thumb while I stalled for an answer. It was clear to Shane and our crew that two things had happened to Dylan over the past month. First, while we were away in Columbus building skills and our friendship, Dylan was back in Troy building muscle but not losing speed. A decent fill-in fullback on short yardage last year, Dylan had become a bulldozer blocker who could also run like a jaguar after a handoff. Mike, Oscar, Ian—nobody who tried for fullback was better. And Dylan's new skills made Shane and Devon look better too. Because teams would fear both backs, they'd pinch the D at the line, and that made Orlando, Terry, and me more dangerous.

"Well? It's a yes-or-no question," Dylan pressed.

And I knew the answer: me, Shane, and the others—we were the Big Five. Dylan would never find a way back in. The silver pole had broken his back. I started to explain all of this to Dylan, tripping over my words like some nervous actor in one of the plays Mom put on.

"Look, Brian, I don't care about Shane or the rest of them except as teammates," Dylan said. "But you and I, bro, we've got a lot of years. Doesn't that count?"

"It would be easier for me, Dylan, if you'd just go along with—"

Dylan shook his head. "I won't tell on you all. But I won't do any more of that Big Six stuff."

I didn't get far in my reply, because Mike suddenly appeared from behind, greeting us both with a way-too-hard back slap. I can't blame him for being angry at us since Dylan and I earned both of the jobs he'd tried out for.

"What's up, Mike?" I said. "Hey, sorry you're not starting, but like last year, maybe somebody—"

"It sucks," Mike said, but he didn't sound that sad or angry. "It would've been so cool."

"Nah," I started, "it's a lot of pressure when you start, because—"

He waved me off. "No, cool to be Big Six. Football's fun, but wow, you guys."

Dylan shook his head. "It's not all that you've heard, trust me."

Mike laughed. "It looks like it's better. Like that Tunnel of Love thing. Lots of us waited by the carnival ride, but what you guys did instead was even better."

Mike grinned and flashed his phone at us. I didn't say a word as I stared at the nude photo of Amber on his screen.

12 / FRIDAY, AUGUST 17— HOME SCRIMMAGE

"Twenty-two red dog. On three, go."

Shane had to shout in the huddle over the roar of the crowd. We had more people watching our first scrimmage than some teams in our division had for homecoming. Mr. Willard had decided to charge admission this year, but it didn't seem to matter.

I took my position on the line and listened intently. Shane told me that during the scrimmage he'd call very few audibles. That way, the coaches would think they were running the offense, but once the season started, Shane said he intended to run and gun.

Shane counted off and took the snap. Twenty-three red dog was our bread-and-butter play, a play as old as football itself: the Lombardi power-option sweep. With me and Dylan providing full-speed-ahead blocking, Devon took the toss and exploded quickly into empty space. If Shane didn't make the toss, he could fake it and run to the other end or fire a flare to Orlando or Terry. It used everybody's strengths, involved both skill and strategy, and made for pure excitement.

My block was still pulling grass out of his helmet once Devon began celebrating in the end zone. With a touchdown on the first play, the fans in the stands came unhinged just like the screen door on Stan's trailer. Which, with the cash I gave him, he could afford to have fixed. But I wondered if any amount of cash would fix what I'd done to Amber.

I joined Devon, Shane, and the rest of the

team near the end zone for the post-score swarm.

Devon patted me and Dylan on our backs. "Great block, guys."

"It's what we do," Dylan said. *We.* I liked the sound of that. Dylan kept his word. We were the Big Five, not six, but he hadn't snitched. Nor had Mike, when I asked him to tell me who'd sent him the photo of Amber. I guess what happened in Big Five *didn't* always stay in Big Five. Was it just Mike with the photo? Everybody on the team? Everybody at school?

"Twelve blue moon on one."

Shane announced in the huddle without enthusiasm as we lined up for the point after. Rather than a quarterback sneak, Coach Whitson called for Dylan to carry the ball. I hit my block perfect, and Dylan knocked down the Dunbar Ducks defensive linemen like he was a bowling ball and they were so many pins. That image made me smile; it helped me remember bowling with Dylan when we were kids. (Although even then, we talked about football, not bowling.)

More congratulations reigned down as the offense left the field. "Good luck," I told Mike as he passed by. He was starting on special teams. He grunted something and ran hard.

Coach Whitson called the backs and ends together on the sideline. "First play and a fifty-yard touchdown. Not bad. Not bad at all." He banged his hand against the clipboard.

"Coach, with this group, we can do it anytime," Shane said. We all laughed until Dylan left the sideline huddle to fix his shoulder pads. "He's not getting the ball again if I can help it."

"But, Shane, he's really good," I said. Devon agreed.

"Look, Oscar's a faster runner," Shane said, "and Ian maybe blocks just as good, so—"

"I need daylight out there," Devon argued. "Oscar can't create that like Dylan can. Not Ian, either."

"Well, I need somebody I can trust to hand the ball to," Shane shot back.

"Just throw it to me," Orlando said.

In fifty seconds, a fifty-yard touchdown had turned into a five-way non-shouting match. It might have gone on for who knows how long had Coach Whitson not interrupted. "Heads up, ladies. Dunbar just fumbled. We got the ball. What do you think? Two touchdowns in less than two minutes!" Coach Whitson shouted. "Time for the Big Six!"

Dylan grabbed his helmet along with the rest of us and started toward the field.

"Wait a second, Dylan," Coach Whitson said sharply. He put his hand on Dylan's arm. "Let's give Ian a chance to run the ball next. It might be his lucky day."

13 / FRIDAY, AUGUST 24—
AWAY SCRIMMAGE

"That had better be a playbook," Coach Z snapped as he walked past me on the bus. I'm not sure why he picked on me. I was probably the only player who had his phone off on the two-hour ride to Xenia. "A scrimmage victory over a weak team like Dunbar don't mean nothing."

I agreed, as I always did with Coach Z, except about one thing. "Coach, this game—can you let Dylan play?"

Coach Z furrowed his thick brow. "Son, the coaches pick the players, not the team."

"I know that. I'm not telling you who to play. It's just—Dylan really wants it."

He squinted at me. "Does he really, Norwood? Does he really?"

Coach walked off before I could answer.

As the bus rolled on, I felt more like I was on a train. From the first jumping jack of conditioning until the last down of the season, football would be a locomotive that pushed everything else aside. I closed my eyes and wondered if the train I rode on—the Big Six Express—had run off the tracks. I'd already ruined Amber's reputation and maybe lost a friend. Could I still jump off safely?

———————————

"By the time we leave tonight, these people will think another tornado tore through their town," Coach Z explained. Xenia, Ohio, was known for two things: a tornado that wiped out most of it, back in the day, and a football program run by a certain former defensive coordinator and assistant at Troy: Coach Ken Zachary, our Coach Z's younger brother. We played in different divisions, so we wouldn't meet during the regular season, only in the playoffs. Playoffs we'd failed to make in the last two years, when Xenia lost in the first round to Athens.

Xenia's stadium was pretty old. There was no bursting out of the tunnel to the cheers of Troy fans who bused over to support their team. Last year's scrimmage with Xenia, at Troy, had been a wild one, with more penalties earned than points. But Coach Z said this year would be different. We'd be disciplined and determined. We'd win, not just because we had the better team with superior coaches and players but because we were better men.

Really, Coach?

Orlando returned the opening kickoff for thirty-five yards, which gave us great field position. Field position we got to know very well as, down after down, Xenia stuffed us. Their D-linemen burst through untouched, so Devon, Ian, and Shane couldn't get going. Shane rarely got time to throw. We had a three-and-out offense.

Our effort was there, but our execution suffered.

By halftime we were down by fourteen. Unlike our fearless leader, who insisted on going for two, the *other* Coach Z believed in kicking for the extra point. During the half, Shane threw a tantrum, yelling at his line but mostly at Ian.

"That's enough!" Coach Z shouted. Shane looked as if he'd been slapped. All preseason he'd been getting away with murder, so maybe it was time for punishment. He deserved it; all of us did. We might have been the team's best athletes, but the Big Five were not better men. No way.

"He's got to put Dylan in," Devon whispered to me between gritted teeth.

Coach Z fumed. "Vince Lombardi said, 'It's easy to have faith in yourself and have discipline when you're a winner, when you're number one. What you got to have is faith and discipline when you're not a winner.' And right now, you are not playing like winners. You're losers."

"We've got to win!" Orlando shouted. "Losing is not an option."

Orlando didn't use the word *we* often, so everybody, myself included, seemed stunned. Pretty soon, Terry and Devon were leading cheers, and the locker room came alive. As we started out toward the field, I pulled Orlando aside. "What's with the newfound spirit?"

Orlando laughed. "Man, if we lose, then we lose it *all*. Get me? As long as we win and make the coaches look good, we can do anything. Do you want to lose all of that?"

We had two minutes left. We needed eighty yards and six points to win. After Ian fumbled twice after the half, Dylan got back in the game. Everything clicked—we marched downfield on a ten-play drive. I did my part not only by throwing vicious blocks but by hauling in a pass on a critical third and five.

"Five seven playmaker split right on three," Shane called and then clapped his hands.

At football camp, I had learned that the hardest thing about being a receiver was not doing anything to tip off your coverage that the play was coming to you. Like any other down where I'd block, I dug my knuckles into the dirt and waited for the count. I pushed by the defensive end, took two hard steps to the left, and then spun like a wheel to get open in the flats. Wide open, so I had plenty of time to watch Shane decide to run the ball, up in the middle, into a Xenia brick wall.

With no time for a huddle, we lined up quickly. Shane called another pass play, one where I provided pass protection. I hit my block while Shane hit Devon in the letters for ten, then fifteen, and finally twenty yards. Xenia scrambled back on defense, and we lined up again.

Shane called a variation of the same play, except the pass went to Dylan, on my side. I raced through my first block and turned it up full blast, knocking them down like a wrecking ball. The months of practices, lifting, skills, and drills matter the most in a game's final minute.

"Twelve dog red three twenty!"

A power sweep, with me and Dylan leading the way, got us twenty-one more yards. First and ten with forty left on the clock. An ill-advised off-tackle run by Devon gained two yards but ate up seconds that we needed. With no time-outs left, Shane called the play that Xenia wouldn't expect. The book said to throw to the wide receivers in the corner of the end zone: make it and it's a TD, miss it and it's a clock stop with time to huddle.

It was a risk, but as I cut into space, turned, and looked up, I knew it would pay off.

———————————

"Nice catch, 75." a Xenia guy said as I stood in the middle of the end zone with the ball cradled against me like a mom with a newborn.

14 / FRIDAY, AUGUST 31—
HOME GAME AND SEASON OPENER

"Brian, everything okay?" Dylan asked. "You hung over or whatever?"

My head hung down, but not for that reason. Shane had limited the parties to Saturday nights since we didn't practice on Sundays. Despite Dylan's fixed role as starting fullback, he'd been clear he wasn't going to be part of the Big Six. Which I respected, but the tone in his voice clearly indicated that he'd lost his respect for me. I always thought he was the toughest guy on the team, but obviously that toughness extended beyond the field. Saying no was so hard and yes was so very easy.

"Party too hard? Too many girls?" Dylan said. "What's wrong with you?"

"I'm fine, Dylan, fine," I lied.

"I don't believe you," he countered and sipped his pregame Dairy Queen milk shake. Everybody needed rituals.

"You're right, it's not fine." I tossed my shake in the trash and went on my way. On the long walk home, I felt like throwing up. I had since the bus ride home from the Xenia game. After hearing the whispers from person to person as the picture moved from phone to phone. "Psst," somebody would say. "I sent you an Amber alert."

As I looked at my phone, I didn't see the picture. Just the missed calls from Amber.

"Son, is everything good?" Dad said as I climbed into the car. Normally, I'd go right from school to a home game, but school had yet to start. The first day brought me a sense of dread I'd not felt in a long time, probably since elementary school, when I didn't know anybody. Now, I'd been to school with some of these people, including Amber, going on eleven years. If I added up everything I'd done wrong in those other years, it wouldn't equal the last two months.

"I'm just a little nervous. You know first game," I answered as I stared out the window.

"Well, you had us all worried in that Xenia game, but that's what happens I guess when . . ." Dad stopped talking and clicked on the radio.

"That's what happens I guess when *what*," I repeated and turned off the radio.

He stayed silent for almost a mile, but then said, "Well, when you break traditions."

"I gave you your money back. I told you we called it off." Five yards for offside truth.

"There are lots of traditions in Troy football, Son. Like the player dinner that Friends of Troy Football hosts before each game," Dad started. By the time we reached the stadium, he'd recounted all of them, even though he understood that I knew these traditions as well as he did.

"Sometimes I wonder if it's all worth it. For some stupid game . . . ," I mumbled.

"Brian, what has gotten into you?" Dad asked. I couldn't tell if he was angry or concerned. Maybe both. "I know it's a lot of pressure, but trust me, it's all worth it. All of it."

You don't know all of it, I thought, and you never can.

"Before I played varsity football, Brian, I was just a stupid kid. I did dumb things and hung around the wrong people. But football, being part of a winning team? That changed everything for me. You just wait. You'll feel the same way soon enough, so have a great game tonight."

"Thanks, Dad." Another father and son might have hugged, but not Big Bill Norwood. Especially since I'd wanted to say, "Dad, you're wrong. I had to join a football team to do dumb things and hang with the wrong people, and no amount of winning will make that better."

"You think something is wrong with Coach Z?" Terry asked as we crowded into the tunnel. I shrugged. "He only quoted Lombardi twice," Terry added. "Maybe he's losing it."

I laughed and gave Terry a high five. But it was me who was losing it, not Coach Z.

In the steel tunnel, the sound of the Troy Central High School marching band seemed deafening. Add onto that all the guys, mostly special teamers like Mike or bench players like Ian, making noise and I'm surprised my eardrums didn't pop. The noise had started earlier with yet another Trojan tradition: cheering parents lining the parking lot, players leaving the lockers for the field.

"Troy, Ohio, are you ready for your hometown heroes?" the PA announcer boomed.

The tunnel shook with the vibrations of a thousand-plus feet stomping and hands clapping. Despite the light at both ends, in the middle of the tunnel, where I stood, it was nearly dark.

"And now your starting offensive squad."

The PA announcer would start with the line; then the ends and backs; and then, finally, he'd end up with Shane.

Near the entrance to the field, my knees buckled from nervousness. Not nervousness at playing in front of my friends, family, and almost every one at school. Not with starting and maybe making a mistake, though I didn't make one in either scrimmage game and very few mistakes in practices. No, my legs would get me on the field and carry me through the battle. I wasn't worried about the field or the game but the faces in the stands.

One face in particular. Amber Murphy. Would she be up there, looking down at me?

I tapped my cleats against the side of the tunnel and the metallic echo shot through my heart. "Starting at tight end, number 75, junior Brian Norwood!"

I burst out of the tunnel. Under my cleats, the perfectly landscaped football field felt like quicksand pulling me down.

15 / MONDAY, SEPTEMBER 3— GAME FILMS

"Norwood, I was impressed. You did double duty. That's very old school."

Coach Colby stood in front of everyone gathered in the school library to watch the game film.

"Like his dad, like Coach Z, and like me," Coach Whitson said. "Everybody used to go both ways back when we played." Coach Whitson seemed clueless as to why everybody was laughing, but I couldn't care less. Nothing was funny, and nothing I did, not even playing the last quarter of our first game in my old linebacker position due to others' injuries, was impressive.

Coach Z's speech half chewed us out and half patted our backs. We'd won by twenty points but scored only eight of those in the second half. "You can't coast, not in this division."

"You're lazy because you're not in the right condition," Coach Colby said. "That's why people got injured. Or should I say, asked to come out of the game. Prepared players are healthy players."

All of us nodded our heads and grunted. Shane had to be the healthiest of all—I'd never seen anybody drink as much orange juice as he did last Saturday night.

"Now, since watching game films is new for a few of you, we're going to break it up. We'll watch the first half, then the Friends are bringing in pizza, and then we'll watch the second half. If you played, take notes. If you didn't play, take even more notes."

More nods, more grunts as the lights went down and Coach Z started his narration of the game, picking apart each play and player. Last year, the films didn't get this detailed treatment, so I wondered what changed. Last year, did Coach Z think we couldn't win? Had he not wanted to waste our time? Or this year, did he think we could win it all and want us over-prepared?

While Shane and the rest of my crew could be heard goofing off when Coach Colby had the floor and the defense was on the field, I paid even closer attention. As great as it was catching the TD pass in the Xenia game and picking up fifty yards receiving in our first game, there was something about tackling. Playing offense was hard work, but after playing both in one game, if only for a short time, I decided D was way harder. It was harder to say no.

"Dylan, you've got to make that block!" Coach Whitson shouted. Dylan had become his whipping boy. If Dylan were on the bench, I bet Whitson would still blame him for a fumble.

"I know, Coach, I know," Dylan said with an

enthusiastic headshake to show he meant it.

"This is a team sport, and if your team-mates can't depend on you to do what's best for the team, well, that's a problem," Coach Z said. "Nobody is bigger than the team. Nobody."

"Did you all hear that?" Coach Whitson said. "There is no *I* in the words *team*, *football*, *Troy*, or *Trojan*!"

Somehow watching twenty-four minutes of playing time took almost two hours. At one point, Coach Z hurled the DVD remote across the room. It hit the wall near Mike's head; he had drawn a penalty on a kick return. By the time the film was over, everybody was hungry, tired, and bored. A bad formula.

"Hey, Coach, do you mind if we go over that last set of downs again, just the backs and the ends?" Shane asked Coach Z. "We can sacrifice hot pizza for a chance to learn."

"Fine," Coach Z said. "The rest of you, make a note. That's leadership."

As soon as the coaching staff and the other players left the Big Five in the library, Orlando shut the door.

"Are we seriously going to watch more game films?" I asked. My stomach growled.

Orlando started giggling. Shane reached into his Troy High football sweatshirt and pulled out something. He walked over to the DVD player, ejected the game disc, and put in another disc. "Mute the volume just in case."

It was good advice. As they watched video Shane had shot of Amber dancing, the other guys bit their lips to stop laughing; I stuffed my right hand in my mouth to stop myself from screaming.

16 / THURSDAY, SEPTEMBER 6—
LAST PRACTICE BEFORE SECOND GAME

"How could you?"

I asked myself that a hundred times, but in my own voice. This was Amber's. I'd be late for practice, which meant staying late afterward—and running the steps—but I deserved all of that and worse.

Since I had PE last hour, Mr. Colby said sure when I asked to leave early to hit the weight room. Not the weight room at school, which was lousy, but the football facility's room. And I didn't exactly lie to him. I was going to lift weights: the weight of shame off my shoulders.

I started to explain, but my words tangled like a rookie hitting the tires. I start, stopped, stumbled, and said nothing. Anything I would've said, Amber was crying too much to hear. I wanted to comfort her, but I knew she thought of me not as a person but as a disease. As we stood in a secluded spot by the unmowed baseball field, I finally found some words.

"Amber, I didn't know," I started. "They didn't tell me everything they'd do with—"

"I don't believe you," she snapped. "It doesn't matter. Everybody knows now. I can tell from how people look at me," she said. "I'm switching schools, and it's your fault. You and your stupid football friends, who think they're so special."

"Amber, it was a stupid bet." I took out my wallet. "I still have some of the money if—"

"If I just shut up? You're making it worse, which I didn't think possible."

More tears from her, more helpless standing a yard away and feeling worthless from me.

"I always thought you were a nice guy," Amber sniffed. "And your mom. Does she know?" I felt sweat break out even in the mid-autumn warmth.

"I don't know," I said.

"Well, she deserves to. Maybe I'll tell her. You, your dad, all of you with your stupid football traditions. Don't you realize none of it matters? None of it! It's just a stupid game with little boys banging their heads together trying to act like men."

I couldn't defend my actions, but I'd stand up for football. "Amber, look, you don't—"

"Shut up, just shut up!" she screamed.

And I knew what I had to do. "Make me!" I said.

When her palm slapped my face, I felt some sense finally sink back into me.

"Where have you been?" Dad asked, more angry than concerned it seemed. "Coach Z said you missed practice without an excuse. You're in big trouble. Big trouble."

I laughed. "But he's not benching me, is he?"

Dad shook his head.

"And you know why? Because I'm Big Six, just like he was. Just like you were."

Dad flinched, as if unsure if "just like you" was an insult or a compliment, so I made it clear. "All of these traditions are so screwed up. They don't amount to anything. They're not about teamwork or sportsmanship or any of that stuff the coaches say. They're the opposite of it."

Dad pointed a finger at me. "How would you know?"

I told him. Everything about what traditions had turned into. Every last detail.

He didn't react much when I told him about the parties—just held a dumb "boys will be boys" expression on his face. He didn't react when I told him about how the coaches treated us differently. Instead, he nodded in approval of the coaches, even the cops, who had let us get away with stuff because we were Big Six.

"That's it?" Dad seemed amused until I told him about Shane's new version of the Tunnel of Love bet and about what happened to Amber.

He seemed to age a year in front of me. "Does Coach Z know about this?"

I shrugged. "He's dropped hints but said nothing directly."

"What are you going to do, Son?" Dad asked.

"I don't know. What should I do?"

He did the hand-on-shoulder thing. "I just hope you don't do something you'll regret."

I swatted his hand away. "Didn't you hear me? I regret all of it."

"I mean like quitting football. That would be a mistake."

"This isn't about football anymore," I said. "This is about everything. This is about who I am."

"You're my son, Brian. That's who you are." He inched closer.

"No, I'm not," I said, "because I'm not Big Six. I'm not one of those guys."

"So what are you going to do?" Dad asked again, softer this time.

"I don't know yet," I answered. "I guess tell Dylan he was right about all of this."

"Whatever you do, let's keep it in the family," Dad whispered. "Trojan Football family."

"That is one messed-up family."

Dad's hand landed back on my shoulder. "Most families are. Even the best ones."

"Even the undefeated state champion ones?"

Dad smiled for the first time.

17 / FRIDAY, SEPTEMBER 7—
BUS RIDE TO AWAY GAME

"Are you sure you want to do this, Brian?" Coach Z asked with Coach Whitson behind his shoulder. Everybody else was on the bus, but I stayed outside. I didn't like being an insider anymore.

"Yes, I don't want to be on the offense. It's not the right place for me. I want to start again at outside linebacker."

"But you're doing so well!" Coach Whitson

shouted. Hadn't they figured it out? It wasn't the offense I wanted to leave; it was the Big Six. I knew I didn't have Dylan's willpower, so escape was my only option.

"Why do you think that I'll start you at linebacker?" Coach Z asked and then started his players-don't-pick-the-team speech again.

While he rambled on, I thought about my choices. Maybe I could blackmail him. I could say "You let me start or else I'll tell everything, and you'll lose five of your best players, your winning season, your reputation, maybe your job."

But that wasn't the person I wanted to be either. I just wanted to play football, plain and simple. I could never make it up to Amber, and I wasn't man enough to walk away from football. I just couldn't. But I could walk away from the Big Six. I could end that part of the legacy. I had no idea if it meant anything, but it was what I could do. My mind replayed those hundreds of linebacker hits again. Maybe after a few hundred high-speed collisions—a few hundred chances to say no!—things would be clearer.

"It's your team, Coach," I said sharply. "But I'm not playing tight end anymore. If that means I sit on the bench, fine. But if you want to win, you'll give me a chance to prove myself."

"Coach Colby would want him to play," Coach Whitson said. Coach Z shook his head.

"Why?" Coach Z asked. "Maybe if I knew why, then I could—"

"You know why," I hissed. "You all know what is going on, and you let it happen. All to win football games that nobody but a few people will remember in a few years. But what I did, what they made me do, well, some of us will live with that for the rest of our lives."

"I don't know what you mean, 75," Coach Z said, acting like he hadn't heard a word I said. And maybe he really hadn't. Maybe he was as blind as I had been. But at least, I felt like I was coming out of the tunnel and into the light.

ABOUT THE AUTHOR

Patrick Jones is the author of more than twenty books for teen readers, including works with a focus on contact sports such as mixed martial arts (The Dojo series), boxing (*The Gamble*), and football (*Out of the Tunnel*). A former librarian for teenagers, Jones won lifetime achievement awards in 2006 from the American Library Association and Catholic Library Association. As a Michigan native and current resident of Minnesota, he's locked into the power battles of the NFC Central, but for him, pro football hasn't been the same since the original Cleveland Browns left Ohio in 1995.

THE RED ZONE

WINNING IS *NOT OPTIONAL.*

OUT of THE TUNNEL

BREAKTHROUGH

THE OPTION

AT ALL COSTS

TAKE AWAY

RISE ABOVE

WELCOME TO THE DOJO

BODY SHOT

HEAD KICK

SIDE CONTROL

TRIANGLE CHOKE

LEARN TO FIGHT, LEARN TO LIVE, AND LEARN TO FIGHT FOR YOUR LIFE.